21

D1258017

EARLY BIRD STORIES™

Teachers in My Community

Bridget Heos Illustrated by **Kyle Poling**

LERNER PUBLICATIONS ◆ MINNEAPOLIS

NOTE TO EDUCATORS

Find text recall questions at the end of each chapter. Critical-thinking and text feature questions are available on page 23. These help young readers learn to think critically about the topic by using the text, text features, and illustrations.

Lerner Publications Company
A division of Lerner Publishing Group, Inc.
241 First Avenue North
Minneapolis, MN 55401 USA

For reading levels and more information, look up this title at www.lernerbooks.com.

Photos on page 22 used with permission of: Monkey Business Images/Shutterstock.com (teachers with students); rawf8/Shutterstock.com (school supplies).

Library of Congress Cataloging-in-Publication Data
Names: Heos, Bridget, author. | Poling, Kyle, illustrator.
Title: Teachers in my community / Bridget Heos ; illustrated by Kyle Poling.
Description: Minneapolis : Lerner Publications, 2019. | Series: Meet a community helper (early bird stories) | Includes bibliographical references and index. | Audience: Age 5-8. | Audience: K to Grade 3.
Identifiers: LCCN 2017052356 (print) | LCCN 2017049676 (ebook) | ISBN 9781541524156 (eb pdf) | ISBN 9781541520226 (lb : alk. paper) | ISBN 9781541527102 (pb : alk. paper)
Subjects: LCSH: Teachers—Juvenile literature.
Classification: LCC LB1775 (print) | LCC LB1775 .H4535 2019 (ebook) | DDC 371.1—dc23

LC record available at https://lccn.loc.gov/2017052356

Manufactured in the United States of America
1-44358-34604-4/3/2018

TABLE OF CONTENTS

We visit Ms. Crawford. She teaches the fourth grade.

"We're learning about animal homes," says Ms. Crawford. Everyone is busy reading and writing.

"Why aren't you teaching?" Molly asks.
"I am," Ms. Crawford says. "I'm teaching them
how to learn by reading."

Ms. Crawford says there are many ways to learn. She teaches the students to learn from one another.

8

They put their animal notes on a whiteboard that connects to a computer. Everyone takes turns sharing.

What are some of the different ways students can learn?

CHAPTER 2

STICKERS AND RED PENS

Ms. Crawford says she learned to be a teacher in college.

"I worked hard," Ms. Crawford tells us. "I want my students to work hard too."

Ms. Crawford shows us a sheet of homework. "One of my jobs is to check my students' work."

"I can tell this student did her best," she says.

"Don't you want your students to make mistakes?" Edward asks. "Then you get to use your red pen."

Ms. Crawford laughs. "No, I want them to get the answers right. That shows me they have learned."

Where do teachers learn to teach?

CHAPTER 3
PAPER CLIPS AND PIZZA PARTIES

Making classroom rules is another part of a teacher's job.

RULES
for Ms. Crawford's Class

★ Be respectful and responsible.

★ Pay attention and follow directions.

★ Raise your hand to speak.

★ Keep hands and feet to yourself.

★ Be prepared for class and ready to learn!

Rules teach students how to be good community members.

"What are these?" asks Jorge. He points to a chain of paper clips.

18

"The class gets paper clips for following our classroom rules," Ms. Crawford says. "When the chain reaches the floor, we have a pizza party."

19

Ms. Crawford rings a bell. It's time for our class to go back to our room.

But first, we give Ms. Crawford a hand!

What are some of the rules for Ms. Crawford's classroom?

21

LEARN ABOUT COMMUNITY HELPERS

Teachers are workers in the community. A community is a group of people who live or work in the same city, town, or neighborhood.

In elementary school, classroom teachers teach most subjects. They often teach math, English, social studies, and science. In middle school and high school, most teachers teach one subject.

Teachers have many classroom tools. They use chalk and markers on chalkboards and whiteboards. Other whiteboards work with a computer. Teachers also have supplies such as pens, pencils, and worksheets. And of course, they have lots of books!

People learning to be teachers are called student teachers. They watch other teachers teach. Then they practice teaching a class themselves.

Teachers never stop learning. They take special classes to learn how to be even better at what they do. There they share ideas about teaching with other teachers.

THINK ABOUT COMMUNITY HELPERS: CRITICAL-THINKING AND TEXT FEATURE QUESTIONS

Why do you think it is important for teachers to learn how to teach?

Why do teachers create classroom rules?

How does this book's front cover tell you what the book is about?

What do the numbers in the bottom corners of the pages tell you?

Expand learning beyond the printed book. Download free, complementary educational resources for this book from our website, www.lernersource.com.

GLOSSARY

college: a school that students go to after they finish high school

community: a group of people who live in the same area

notes: writings about what a person read, learned, saw, or heard

subject: an area of learning, such as math or science

TO LEARN MORE

BOOKS

Parkes, Elle. *Hooray for Teachers!* Minneapolis: Lerner Publications, 2017. Check out this book to learn more about what teachers do.

Yankovic, Al. *My New Teacher and Me!* Illustrated by Wes Hargis. New York: Harper, 2013. Read this fun story about Billy and his new teacher.

WEBSITE

Teacher Acrostic Poem
http://www.enchantedlearning.com/poetry/acrostic/teacher/
Visit this website to print out a page where you can write a poem for your teacher.

INDEX